James Brown

by Jennifer Fandel

Raintree

Chicago, Illinois

For information, address the publisher:
Raintree, 100 N. LaSalle, Suite 1200, Chicago, IL 60602

Printed and bound in the United States at Lake Book Manufacturing, Inc.
07 06 05
10 9 8 7 6 5 4 3 2

Library of Congress Cataloging-in-Publication Data:

Fandel, Jennifer.
  James Brown / Jennifer Fandel.
    v. cm. -- (African-American biographies)
Includes bibliographical references (p.   ) and index.
Contents: Childhood -- Finding his talent -- A teenager in trouble -- Starting over -- The big break -- A musical pioneer -- The civil rights movement -- Trying times -- Rebirth -- Recognition.
  ISBN 0-7398-7027-0 (library binding-hardcover) -- ISBN 1-4109-0317-6 (pbk.)
  1. Brown, James, 1928---Juvenile literature. 2. Singers--United States--Biography--Juvenile literature. 3. African American singers--Biography--Juvenile literature. [1. Brown, James, 1928- 2. Singers. 3. Soul music. 4. African Americans--Biography.] I. Title. II. Series: African American biographies (Chicago, Ill.)
  ML3930.B87F36 2003
  782.421644'092--dc20

2003001509

Acknowledgments
The publishers would like to thank the following for permission to reproduce photographs:
pp. 4, 48 Lynn Goldsmith/Corbis; pp. 6, 58 AFP/Corbis; p. 8 Hulton-Deutsch Collection/Corbis; pp. 10, 11, 14, 38, 40, 46, 56 Bettmann/Corbis; pp. 12, 16, 27, 43, 44 Library of Congress; p. 18 Neal Preston/Corbis; pp. 22, 28, 30 Hulton/Archive by Getty Images; p. 25 Ethan Miller/Corbis; p. 32 Mosaic Images/Corbis; p. 34 Contemporary African Art Collection Limited/Corbis; p. 50 S.I.N./Corbis; p. 52 Corbis Sygma; p. 54 Reuters NewMedia Inc./Corbis.

Cover photograph: Neal Preston/Corbis

Some words are shown in bold, **like this.** You can find out what they mean by looking in the glossary.

Contents

James Brown is known for his great voice and fantastic dance moves. These talents led James to become known as the Godfather of Soul and one of the greatest entertainers the world has ever heard or seen.

Introduction

Music was never the same after James Brown danced and sang his way into the music scene. Audiences were amazed at his performances. He moved his feet in ways people had never seen before. He slid easily across the floor. He did splits. By the end of a performance, sweat soaked his clothes and his voice was hoarse. A performance by James Brown was not something that others could easily imitate. This hardworking, talented man was an original.

James Brown stands out among American musicians for his contributions to modern popular music. He helped develop **soul music,** and he started a new kind of music called **funk.** Soul music is a form of African-American music that contains a lot of emotion. Funk is a form of African-American music where all the instruments pick up the beat. He also inspired future musicians who played rock and roll, disco, and rap music. Everything that James heard fueled his music. And everything James played fueled the music of other musicians.

In July 2002, James performed at the Paleo Music Festival in Nyon, Switzerland. He was 69 years old and a legend in his own time.

James Brown also left his mark by helping others. He grew up poor and went to school through only the seventh grade. His rags-to-riches story has been an example to many people. He felt that his success put him in a position to help others. He was active in the **Civil Rights Movement.** This was the struggle for African Americans to gain the rights that are guaranteed to all U.S. citizens. He has dedicated his life to spreading messages about education and business ownership. James Brown was one of the most popular musicians ever to mix his political ideas and his social beliefs with his music.

James Brown will continue to be remembered for his combination of inventive music, energetic performances, and social messages. He is a musical pioneer who dared to go where few had gone before. For that, he has earned a special place in the history of music.

In his own words

"When I do my music, I include a lot of people, but nobody's really involved except myself. Just God and me. I guess I'm like Einstein— let 'em worry about my theory after I'm dead."

This is James in 1973. He was already famous and known as the Godfather of Soul.

Chapter 1: Rough Beginnings

James knew hardship from the moment he was born. James Joe Brown Jr. was born on May 3, 1933, to Joe and Susie Brown. His parents were poor and lived in a one-room cabin in the woods outside Barnwell, South Carolina. James's father went to school through only the second grade. He made up for his lack of schooling by working hard, often nearly all day and all night. In fact, James's father rarely went a day without working. But he often had to look hard and travel far to find work. When James was young, his father's job was to tap pine trees to make turpentine. Turpentine is oil made from pine trees that is used to remove paint.

Life became even harder when James was four. His mother moved away and left James and his father behind. They learned to survive together without her. They lived in rough workers' camps and ate whatever was cheap and easy to cook. They ate black-eyed peas, lima beans, corn bread, and greens that they picked in the woods.

James lived with his father in a workers' camp much like this one when he was four and five years old.

At ages four and five, James spent most of his time alone. He was very lonely. James's Aunt Minnie soon came to live with James and his father. But that did not help James's loneliness. His father was at work most of the time. Aunt Minnie was often busy taking care of the household. James did not have any playmates because he lived so far out in the country. Because of this, he learned at an early age to entertain and depend on himself.

James Brown's hit singles

1956: "Please Please Please"
1958: "Try Me "
1960: "Think"
1962: "Night Train"
1964: "Out of Sight"
1965: "Papa's Got a Brand New Bag
1965: "I Got You (I Feel Good)"
1966: "It's a Man's Man's Man's World"
1966: "Don't Be a Dropout"
1967: "Cold Sweat"
1968: "I Got the Feelin'"
1968: "Say It Loud, I'm Black and I'm Proud"
1968: "America Is My Home"
1969: "Give It Up or Turn It a Loose"
1969: "I Don't Want Nobody to Give Me Nothing"
1970: "Super Bad"
1970: "Get Up, Get Into It, and Get Involved"
1971: "Soul Power"
1972: "Talkin' Loud and Sayin' Nothing"
1972: "Get on the Good Foot"
1974: "The Payback"
1974: "Funky President (People It's Bad)"
1985: "Living in America"

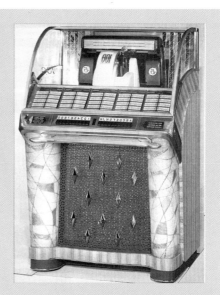

James went to school at a time when schools were segregated. All of the other children in his class were African American. White and black children were not allowed to attend school together.

Moving to Georgia

When James was five, he moved with his father and his Aunt Minnie to Augusta, Georgia. This was an even rougher place, but it was the best that James's father could do. James's Aunt Honey rented out rooms in her house, and the three of them moved in with her. James's father found better work around Augusta, but he soon left and never lived with James and Aunt Minnie again. He visited sometimes, and he provided what he could for James.

One advantage to James's new life in Georgia was that he had someone to play with, his cousin. Junior was Aunt Honey's son. The cousins were as close as brothers, and they were often called Little Junior and Big Junior. James was Little Junior. A small boy, he was the little kid wherever he went.

Fighting to survive

James got teased at school for being smaller than the rest of the kids. He had already had a tough life, but the teasing made him tougher. Sometimes, James felt angry about being poor. His teachers sent him home from school many times because he was not dressed properly. He felt helpless when this happened. James did not have other clothes, and he had no way of getting the clothes his teacher wanted him to wear. He did not like missing school and began to act out his anger. He got into fights and stole classmates' lunches.

James figured out what he needed to do to survive when he was just a child. In 1940 soldiers arrived in Augusta to train for military service at Fort Gordon. That was a military base in Augusta. James saw that all these new people started coming to town and he got an idea. He could make some money by entertaining and working for the soldiers. James began to make up his own dances and perform them in the streets. He also delivered groceries and shined shoes on street corners. The soldiers rewarded him with coins. He brought this money home to his Aunt Honey to help pay the rent.

James sang and performed at this 1978 concert. He first started making music when he was five years old.

Chapter 2:
Finding His Talent

James's interest in music started at a very young age, perhaps as a way to deal with his loneliness. When James was five, his father gave him a harmonica. At age six, James's father brought home an organ with a missing leg. His father propped it up, and James sat down at it immediately. That afternoon, he taught himself a song. All of the rough people in Aunt Honey's house gathered around and listened to this young boy play. From that moment on, James knew that he loved music.

He also listened to all of the music that he could. He heard most of this music on the radio and on records at home. He listened to **gospel, jazz,** and **rhythm and blues (R & B).** Gospel music is a type of religious music. Jazz is lively music that is often **improvised,** or made up as it is played. African Americans developed both gospel and jazz music. R & B is a kind of fast

Count Basie was seated at his piano in this 1958 photo. In the 1950s, Basie was a popular singer.

dance music, also developed by black musicians. James also loved listening to pop musicians, including Frank Sinatra, Count Basie, and Bing Crosby. "Pop" music is short for "popular" music.

A love of performance

James first saw musical performances at church. On most Sundays, an old man from his neighborhood asked James to help him get to church. This brought James to church often.

James was captivated by the performance that the preacher put on every Sunday. The preacher shouted his message with emotion. He fell to his knees and acted as if he were exhausted or praying really hard. As a child, James copied many of the preacher's moves. These became an important part of his later stage performances.

On stage

At the age of eleven, James gave his first performance. He entered an **amateur**-night contest at the Lenox Theatre in Augusta. An amateur is someone who is not a professional at whatever he or she is doing. James won first prize for singing a popular song of the day, "So Long." After that, he entered every amateur contest that he could, and he often won.

James started his first band, the Cremona Trio, when he was thirteen. The band members borrowed old instruments from their school. The Cremona Trio played together for three years. They performed at amateur contests and fund-raisers for their school.

James is such an energetic performer that sometimes his perfectly styled hair gets out of place.

Chapter 3:
A Teenager in Trouble

The first song James wrote seemed to predict the future. He wrote the song "Goin' Back to Rome" during his early teenage years with the Cremona Trio. It was about the town of Rome, Georgia, which had a prison. The song was fitting for what lay ahead.

James always cared about his appearance and wanted to look good. This was especially important to him because he had grown up so poor. He remembered those shameful times at school when he did not have proper clothes. He began stealing so that he could have the kind of clothes he wanted. Soon, his stealing grew into a habit. He stole everything he could. His cousin Junior begged him to stop stealing. Junior could see that James's habit would get him into trouble.

James Brown's sense of style

When James was in elementary school, he was sent home for not having the right clothes. That had a lasting affect on him. After that, James always cared about looking good and being fashionable. This did not stop even after he was sent to the **juvenile detention center.** He hated the baggy prison pants he had to wear. At his job in the laundry, James would exchange his baggy pants for new ones that fit him better. Eventually, his **supervisors** found out about his trick and put a stop to it. A supervisor is someone who watches over and directs the work of other people. But James just could not bear those baggy pants. Instead, he put starch into his pants and ironed stiff creases into them. James stood out from the rest of the inmates in his starched uniform. This bothered his supervisors, but they finally gave up. They realized he just had to be different.

The police were soon on James's trail. He dodged them when he went out stealing. But when James was fifteen, the police caught up with him. He was sent to a juvenile detention center in Rome, Georgia, in 1949. A juvenile detention center is like a prison for teenagers. He never went back to school after he was arrested. He had only attended school through the seventh grade.

Reform through music

At the center, James formed a **gospel** quartet with three other boys. The members of the quartet gave James the name "Music Box." They did not have instruments, so they made their own. They played a washtub bass and drums made out of old metal tubs. James made a small guitar out of a wooden box and some string.

The detention center was moved to Toccoa, Georgia, around this time. In Toccoa, the band was asked to perform at events in the community. They sang at nursing homes and any other place where people had requested a little gospel music to brighten the day.

James was well liked and trusted by his supervisors and fellow inmates. This trust was tested one day when the band performed at a nursing home. The band members were singing their hearts out. They liked to make people happy. While they played, the guard from the detention center forgot about the inmates and went home. Later, the people who ran the detention center realized that the inmates were gone. They rushed to the nursing home. They figured the inmates would be gone. But they were still there, still singing.

The people who ran the detention center taught James a lot of important lessons. Many were kind to James and helped him become a better person. A few were like fathers to James. Throughout his life, James kept in touch with many of the people there who had helped shape him.

After leaving the detention center, James continued to make music. By 1955, he and his bandmates were becoming well known throughout the South. He had this studio photo taken when the band was gaining popularity.

Chapter 4: Starting Over

At age nineteen, James wrote to the parole board. A parole board is a group of people who decide whether a prisoner should be freed before the end of his or her sentence. James had been in the detention center for three years. He believed he had changed for the better. He wanted a chance to sing gospel music professionally. The parole board knew how talented he was. They also knew how much James's **supervisors** liked and trusted him.

The parole board decided to give James a chance. They granted his release, but he was not allowed to go back to Augusta. He had to stay in Toccoa so they could keep an eye on him. He found a sponsor family to take him in until he could get on his feet. A sponsor is someone who supports someone else, often with food, shelter, or money. A Toccoa family named the Byrds volunteered to be James's sponsor family.

Gospel music

James started singing **gospel** music wherever he could. He sang in church with the Byrd family, and he sang with one of the Byrd's daughters, Sarah. The duo made guest appearances in area churches.

Soon, James and Sarah paired up with two other singers to form the group the Ever Ready Gospel Singers. James thought this might be his musical opportunity. In 1952 they made a recording of the gospel song "His Eye Is on the Sparrow." They drove all the way to Nashville, Tennessee, to ask a radio station to play it. But the station rejected their song. The saddened group drove back to Georgia.

Rhythm and blues

Now James moved away from gospel music. He began playing **rhythm and blues (R & B)**. He joined Sarah's brother Bobby's band, which was called the Toccoa Band. Other than a piano, they did not have many instruments. The band members kept the beat by stomping their feet. They filled up the room by singing loud.

The band used tricks to get an audience when they toured the local towns. They often brought as many people as they could fit into their old car. In order to come along, their friends had to promise to be in the audience and make a lot of noise. The band also pulled the

James dances while singing at a concert in 1998. Early in his career, it was apparent that James could really entertain his audience.

room's curtains shut or put dark paper over the windows. This made people curious. They came in to see what was happening.

Soon, there was a problem within the band. Bobby realized that much of James's talent was not being used. James knew how to entertain an audience. He was a great singer, and he could really dance. Byrd and James decided that James would be the lead singer of the band. But other band members were hurt by the decision.

Many of them threatened to quit, but their parents talked them into staying. The parents recognized James's talent and thought the band would go far with him as the lead singer.

Meanwhile, James had something else to be excited about. In 1953 James's personal life changed dramatically. He married a woman from Toccoa, Velma Warren. He and Velma would have three sons together. But their marriage ended in divorce, probably because James was away from home so much.

Small success

The Toccoa Band began to see some rewards. They saved the money they earned from their performances. With it they ordered an electric guitar and a very small amplifier through the mail. An amplifier is a piece of electronic equipment that makes the sound of an instrument louder. They put together a drum set out of old drums from the high school.

The band began to get more professional. They often traveled to Greenville, South Carolina, to watch professional bands and learn from them. Around the same time, they had chances to practice what they had learned. The band was invited to play tea parties. These were events held in Toccoa's downtown in the middle of the day. These performances attracted the whole town. This was James's first exposure to a white audience. The year was 1954, and the band was performing as the Flames.

James and his band played a lot of concerts. Much of their early popularity came from this constant touring.

James' voice, dance moves, and natural musical talents were impossible to ignore and he soon became the leader of the Flames. James directs the band from his piano during this practice session, while Bobby Byrd stands, resting his hand on the piano.

Chapter 5:
The Big Break

In the mid-1950s, the Flames were getting closer to fame. They toured almost constantly, and their popularity throughout the South gave them hope. They moved to Macon, Georgia, to make more connections with people in the music business. There they met the singer Little Richard. Little Richard was very popular in the South, and his popularity was growing quickly. He decided to move to California, where he would later record his nationwide hits "Tutti Frutti" and "Good Golly, Miss Molly." Little Richard canceled all of his southern performances when he moved. That is where James came in.

James was asked to take over Little Richard's performances. He worked with Little Richard's band and pretended that he was Little Richard. On stage, he did not say that he was James Brown. But he did perform some of his own songs. His performances convinced a talent scout at King Records to sign the Flames to a recording deal.

Little Richard

One of the first rock and roll musicians, Little Richard was born Richard Penniman in 1932 in Macon, Georgia. As a child Richard sang **gospel** music at his church and learned to play the saxophone and the piano. He began to record music in 1951. His energetic music combined gospel with R & B.

In 1955 Little Richard recorded "Tutti Frutti." It was his first hit. Then came a string of others, including "Long Tall Sally," "Lucille," and "Good Golly, Miss Molly." Little Richard began to give wild performances across the country. Audiences loved it. Little Richard wore wild outfits, and screamed while he banged on his piano.

In 1959 Little Richard temporarily quit rock and roll to devote himself to a religious life. He recorded gospel songs and preached the stories of the Bible. In 1962 he went back to performing rock and roll and by 1968, he had sold 32 million records. In 1986 he was inducted into the Rock and Roll Hall of Fame. Although Little Richard has retired, this legend of music still makes occasional appearances on television.

Attracting attention

King Records' owner, Syd Nathan, did not like the Flames' work when he first heard it. He almost refused to record them. Then he changed his mind and they recorded the song "Please Please Please." But Nathan was still unsure about the Flames. He did not want to release the song to the public. Finally, after months of holding onto the song, the record label finally released "Please Please Please" in 1956. It eventually sold 1 million copies, and it became King Records' best-selling single of all time. A single is a record that just has one song on it.

The Flames' success caught the eye of Ben Bart. He ran Universal Attractions, a **booking company,** in New York. A booking company sets up performances for bands to play. Bart had seen the Flames perform and was amazed by James's singing and dancing. He became their **agent.** This meant he looked for business opportunities for the band. Bart was also James's manager for many years. He was like a father to James, who gave him the nickname "Pop." Bart spent most of his free time touring with James and the band.

Bart decided that James needed to be recognized as the leader of the band. To achieve this, he changed their name from the Flames to James Brown and the Famous Flames. This new name caused a lot of anger in the band. Almost all of the band members quit when they heard the news.

Around this time, Little Richard quit performing so he could devote his life to religion. James was asked to take over his performances again. But this time he did not pretend that he was Little Richard. He toured as himself.

Try me

James put together a new group of musicians to replace the band members who had quit. For James Brown and the Famous Flames,

In the 1960s and 1970s, the Apollo Theater could make or break a new band. The Apollo was and remains a landmark of New York City's Harlem neighborhood.

the music business was hard between 1956 and 1958. They recorded a lot of music, but it was unsuccessful on the **record charts.** These charts measure how popular a song is. Syd Nathan did not want them to record anything else. He thought their new career might be coming to an end.

But the band drew large, enthusiastic crowds when they toured the South. James always performed a song that he had written called "Try Me." The crowds loved the song, but Syd Nathan refused to record it. Nathan changed his mind when he found out that there were thousands of requests for that song. In 1958 "Try Me" went to number one on the **R & B** chart.

A showman in the making

In April of 1959, James's success led him to New York City's Apollo Theater. This theater was in New York's Harlem neighborhood. It was probably the most important place an African-American entertainer could perform. The Apollo's audience was serious about their entertainment. Their reaction to a performer could determine a performer's future. They would boo a performer off the stage for a poor performance or applaud wildly for a good one.

The Apollo needed a lot of people to perform. There were six performances every day at the Apollo. The performances were short, though, since so many people performed at each show.

James wanted his show to stand out from the competition. He danced up a storm, dripped sweat, and sang until it seemed his voice would go out. The crowd loved him. The band ended with its first hit, "Please Please Please." The crowd went wild.

James Brown and the Famous Flames were successful in their first appearance at the Apollo. But James promised himself that he would soon be the Apollo's top act.

James knew a live album of his shows at the Apollo would become a best-seller. He was right. People everywhere, including these women in Mali, a country in western Africa, snatched it up.

Chapter 6:
A Musical Pioneer

In December of 1959, James was invited back to the Apollo for a second time. He became the top act the third time he played at the Apollo. This time, he wanted to do something extra special. The audiences at the Apollo were tough. They expected better every time. With this in mind, he developed the *James Brown Revue*. This was a show with many musical acts, comedians, dancers, and his solo performances. The *James Brown Revue* was a success, and it drew huge crowds. Lines formed down the street as people waited to see the show.

He was invited back to the Apollo just three months later. Fans were waiting in long lines on a cold and snowy February day. James got an idea when he heard about all of the people waiting outside. He and the band went out and talked to people in the line and thanked them for coming. They poured each person a cup of coffee to warm them up while they waited.

The Apollo

The Apollo Theater is a landmark of Harlem, New York. Harlem is the historically African-American section of New York City. In 1934 it opened on 125th Street as a theater for black entertainers. Night after night, performances began with the phrase, "It's show time at the Apollo!"

Entertainers saw performing at the Apollo Theater as their chance to break into stardom. On Wednesday nights, the Apollo held a competition called **Amateur Night**. Many would-be singers, dancers, comedians, and actors competed in the Amateur Nights.

The Apollo was a place where many African-American entertainers established their reputations. Its audiences were hard to impress and had high expectations. Wild applause at the Apollo meant a lot to performers. Many performers, including James Brown, liked the demanding audiences. They made them work hard and perform better.

In 1977 the Apollo closed due to money problems. Its neon lights no longer brightened the street. Performers wondered if their names would ever appear again on the sign out front. Their fans wondered the same thing.

In 1981 a group of people bought the Apollo Theater. They began restoring it to its old brilliance. The Apollo reopened in 1985 much to the delight of performers and fans. Today, the Apollo continues to be a place where performers of color, as well as some white performers, make their reputations.

Live at the Apollo

James wanted to record a live album after the success of the Apollo shows. But live albums were not common at the time. Record companies did not like making them because they were expensive. James was sure a *Live at the Apollo* album would be a huge success. Syd Nathan at King Records thought differently. He refused to record it. So James used his own money to record the album in October of 1962. He even paid for audience members' tickets if they promised to make a lot of noise and have a good time. Their voices were loud and enthusiastic on the album.

Live at the Apollo was a huge success when the album was released in January of 1963. A surprised Nathan had to say that he was wrong. The album changed the audience for James. He was no longer playing only for African-American audiences. He had the attention of all Americans. He had a young, white audience that was drawn to the **rhythm and blues** sound. But white radio stations would not play the album. This made James's success with young whites even more amazing. They were finding out about the album by word of mouth, and by listening to African-American radio stations. James had officially crossed over to an audience that he never thought he could get.

Funk

In 1965 James Brown and the Famous Flames started to develop a new kind of music. It was called **funk.** This music centered on **rhythm,** or steady beat, as the most important part of the music.

James was reaching an incredible number of people with his music by 1967. He was popular with both African-American and white audiences.

James's musicians had always paid close attention to the bass guitar and the drums. But soon they began experimenting with finding a rhythm in every instrument. They ended up with music that sounded much different from the other music of the time. Some people called it the James Brown Sound. Audiences got their first taste of **funk** with James's 1965 song "Papa's Got a Brand New Bag."

James's style of recording and making new music also changed during this time. Many of his songs were now **improvised.** He and his band performed in the studio with the same energy as they performed onstage. The recordings had the feel of a live performance.

This new music brought the band more success. "Papa's Got a Brand New Bag" was the band's second chart-topper. The song won James a Grammy Award for best **R & B** performance. A Grammy is an award given for the best songs and albums of that year. The new sound was a hit in the United States, and it soon became an international hit. People everywhere were enjoying this unique sound.

James was reaching a huge national audience through his live and televised performances. He appeared on the television music and entertainment shows *American Bandstand* and the *Ed Sullivan Show.* He performed in a concert movie called *The T.A.M.I. Show.* T.A.M.I. stood for Teen Age Music International. These appearances made him even more popular with both white and African-American audiences. He also began performing huge shows at stadiums and concert halls. In 1967 he released "Cold Sweat," another hit funk song.

On December 24, 1970, James appeared on The Dick Cavett Show, *a popular talk and entertainment show. By then, he was known as Soul Brother Number One.*

Chapter 7:
The Civil Rights Movement

Throughout the 1960s, the lives of African Americans continued to be very hard. Places in the South were **segregated,** or separated, according to race because some white people wanted it that way. African Americans were treated very poorly in this separated society. They were not allowed to attend the same schools as white people. Black people could not sit at the same lunch counters as white people to eat. Instead, everything was labeled. Water fountains had signs saying "Colored Only" and "Whites Only." Public bathrooms were labeled the same way. Usually, the schools, hospitals, and other things that black people could use were not as good as those for white people. And sometimes, there simply were no water fountains, bathrooms, or places to eat for African Americans.

James had experience with **segregation** in his years with the Flames. In the South, the Flames could not use public restrooms in white areas. They were not always served in restaurants or allowed to stay in motels. James did not like this. But he did not think there was anything he could do to change it.

James's thoughts on this changed when the band stopped at a bus station for lunch one day. They sat and ate at the African-American section of the lunch counter. Then something surprising happened. Some young African Americans and whites came in and sat down in the "wrong" areas. These people were trying to end **segregation** by holding **protests** at lunch counters and on buses throughout the South. They were known as Freedom Riders.

James had been very busy with his music. He had not known that such a huge change was taking place. Now, in the bus station, he watched whites attack the Freedom Riders. They pushed and punched them. The band became afraid. They got out of there as fast as they could.

That day in the bus station was an important one for James. He realized that achieving fame was not a great enough goal. He felt he had a responsibility to other African Americans. People listened to him sing on stage. He now thought they might listen to his ideas, too. He would use his fame to change people's ideas and actions. He did this slowly, through his music.

A message through music

James had more control over his performances as he became more popular. He was scheduled to play a show in Augusta, Georgia. He was excited to play in his hometown. But then he found out that the show would be **segregated.** Most of the seats were reserved for

Many people participated in the Civil Rights Movement of the 1950s and 1960s. Some African Americans, such as those pictured, used sit-ins to protest segregation.

whites. A few African-Americans were allowed to sit in the balcony. James tried to stop the show's segregation. But he ran into too many obstacles. From that moment on, he vowed never to play a segregated show again.

James's next show was in Macon, Georgia. He told officials that the show had to be **integrated,** which means that people of any color would be welcome. The town's officials decided to not mention that to the audience. They would wait and see what

James Meredith was an important civil rights activist. He was the first African American to attend Mississippi State University. James visited Meredith in the hospital after Meredith was shot during a protest.

happened. African Americans and whites came to see the show and stood next to one another. There were no fights and no trouble. People got along just fine when they sat together. All people enjoyed listening to James Brown's music.

Lifting spirits

During the 1950s and 1960s, people in the **Civil Rights Movement** were very active. They worked to get **segregation** replaced with **integration,** or the mixing of races in public places.

Efforts to end segregation were often met with violence. African Americans were beaten and killed for fighting for their rights.

At first, James just became a cheerleader for the cause. In 1966 he visited a man named James Meredith in the hospital. Meredith had been the first student to integrate the all-white Mississippi State University in 1962. Now, he had been shot and wounded during a peaceful march for voting rights in Tupelo, Mississippi. James also put on a show for the marchers in Tupelo. He knew they needed their spirits raised.

Responsibility

James gradually became a spokesperson for the Civil Rights Movement. He tried to use his connections to help make change. He made many calls to President Lyndon Johnson and Vice-President Hubert Humphrey to tell them how people felt. He also spoke with Dr. Martin Luther King Jr. often. King was a well-known civil rights leader.

In 1966 James began to encourage education through the Don't Be a Dropout campaign. He presented his campaign ideas and the song "Don't Be a Dropout" to Vice President Hubert Humphrey. Humphrey supported the project. James started a newsletter and Don't Be a Dropout clubs for kids. He also encouraged adults to go back to school to get their general education degree (GED). He gave $500 scholarships to high school students to use for college. In six months, he gave out more than 500 scholarships.

In 1968 James and Vice President Hubert Humphrey spoke to 500 children in Los Angeles. They encouraged the children to stay in school.

James also believed that gaining business skills would help African Americans. In 1968 he bought his first radio station in Knoxville, Tennessee. At the time, there were 500 radio stations in the United States aimed at African-American audiences. But only five of those were owned by African Americans. James used his radio station to train African Americans in advertising, programming, and management. He bought two more stations, in Baltimore and in Augusta, and set up more training programs. The Augusta station was one that James knew well. He used to shine shoes in front of it as a boy.

Calming the storm

James used his position to help calm a lot of bad situations. In 1966 and 1967, **riots** broke out throughout the United States. A riot is a crowd of people that behaves in a noisy, violent, and out-of-control way. The largest of these riots happened on April 4, 1968. That was the day Martin Luther King Jr. was killed. Rioting broke out in the major cities. Many people were injured, some were killed, and many businesses were destroyed.

James was stunned and angry that King had been shot. But he wanted to calm the rioting. James did not believe in violence as a way to solve problems. He understood why people were angry. But he believed in peaceful **protest.** He broadcast messages on his radio stations. He asked people to stay calm and peaceful out of respect for King. His messages did not stop the rioting. But they did make people stop and think about their actions, and how they were not what King would have wanted.

Some of the worst rioting happened in Washington, D.C. James went there to talk with the rioters. He spoke on television. The president's wife, Lady Bird Johnson, called James at home to say thank you. He was invited to a White House dinner. A note waited for him at his seat. It was a thank-you card from President Johnson.

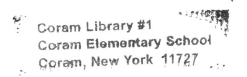

James continued performances such as this one in the 1970s, even though people had begun to protest and even threaten him. He did stop performing for a time in the early 1970s, but quickly returned.

Chapter 8:
Trying Times

In 1968 James released two songs that made people very angry. "America Is My Home" was written in honor of the United States. He sang this song when he toured Vietnam during the war. People in the military thought it was a song about American pride. But many African Americans thought the song was about pride in the U.S. government. They saw no reason to feel pride in their government. They felt it had let them down in their struggle for **civil rights.**

James also released "I'm Black and I'm Proud." This song angered some of James's white audiences. Some African Americans believed that they would achieve equality only by violence. Whites heard James's song as a cry for more of this violence. As a result, white radio stations stopped playing all of his music.

Bobby Byrd, shown here on the right, was James's longtime friend and bandmate. He left James Brown and the Flames in 1973 to pursue a solo career.

James felt torn between his political beliefs and his music. Political means involved with the debate and activity of governing a country. He campaigned for politicians, including Hubert Humphrey and Richard Nixon. This made many of his fans angry. They felt Humphrey and Nixon were not strong supporters of **civil rights.** Plus, both Humphrey and Nixon supported the war.

People expressed their anger with James. Every time he performed, they formed picket lines to **protest** his political ideas. A picket line is a line of people protesting something they do not like. People in these lines often hold signs. James lost a lot of popularity during this time. But he felt it was worth it.

Sometimes people threatened James because of his beliefs. One time someone left a grenade with his name on it outside his hotel room. A grenade is a small, exploding weapon that can be thrown. It was not a real grenade, but it encouraged him to be careful. In 1970 James decided to retire from giving live performances. He later changed his mind because he missed it so much.

Personal challenges

Suddenly, James felt as if he were losing everyone close to him. First his manager, Ben Bart, died in 1968. His death was like the loss of a father. Syd Nathan, the owner of King Records, also died in 1968. Then James's oldest son, Teddy, died in a car accident in New York in 1973. Finally, James's longtime friend and musical partner Bobby Byrd left the band in 1973. He wanted to pursue an independent music career. For a while, James did not know if he could go on performing. But he decided to keep working and found that work was a way of healing.

He also felt that he was losing touch with his audiences. In 1975 disco music became popular. It was played on records in dance clubs. This trend hurt musicians who gave live performances. James cut back on his U.S. performances. Instead, he played in Europe and Africa, where his music was still popular. But he refused to perform in South Africa. Whites in South Africa practiced apartheid. Apartheid means that the white South Africans controlled the people of color through segregation and other ways.

James was offered a role in the 1980 Blues Brothers *movie. He also appeared in the sequel,* The Blues Brothers 2000. *The 1998 taping of the sequel is shown here. James is on the right.*

Chapter 9: Rebirth

In 1980 unexpected opportunities came for James. The comedians John Belushi and Dan Ackroyd wanted James to be in their movie *The Blues Brothers*. Then, the variety show *Saturday Night Live* invited him to perform. A new, younger generation saw James in the movie and became interested.

Suddenly James Brown was back in style. He got back in touch with his audience by performing at these small clubs. People began demanding performances of his old songs.

Then, in 1986, James recorded the song "Living in America" for the movie *Rocky IV*. "Living in America" won him a Grammy for Best Male **R & B** Performance. The younger generations, who had not heard about him when they were growing up, thought he was amazing. They wanted to know more about this exciting performer and his original music.

On October 20, 2000, James performed with Lenny Kravitz at the 2000 VH1 Vogue Fashion Awards in New York City. James was and continues to be an important influence on other musicians.

His musical influence

Musicians had always been interested in James's music. He influenced British bands such as the Rolling Stones in the 1960s. But in the 1980s, a new generation of musicians began studying his music and copying his dancing. He had a huge effect on Michael Jackson and Prince. Both brought a lot of energy to the stage, and they danced constantly. They learned a lot from James. In fact, Prince once lay on the floor backstage during a show to watch James's feet. Prince later asked him if he was wearing roller skates. Prince thought that was the only way James could make his moves so fast and smooth. Prince's music is also influenced by James's pioneering work with **funk** music.

Rap musicians also used James as inspiration. They began using the rhythms of James's music for their own songs by sampling his songs. Sampling is when musicians take a sound from an older song and use it to create a musical effect in a new song. James was honored that people wanted to use his songs, but he thought rap musicians should have to pay to use other people's songs. Eventually, an arrangement was made so that artists were paid for the samples taken from their music.

In his own words

"Don't terrorize. Organize. Don't burn.
Give kids a chance to learn.
The real answer to race problems in
this country is education. Not burning
and killing. Be ready. Be qualified. Own
something. Be somebody. That's black power."
(From a speech given during the Washington, D.C., riots, 1968.)

On January 23, 1986, James became one of the first three musicians inducted into the Rock and Roll Hall of Fame. Pictured with James is Jerry Lee Lewis and Fats Domino.

Chapter 10:
Recognition

In the late 1980s, people began recognizing James for his achievements in music. In 1986 he was inducted into the Rock and Roll Hall of Fame. He was one of the first 10 musicians to be inducted. In 1992 he received an Award of Merit from the American Music Awards. In 1993 he was given a Lifetime Achievement Award at the Grammy Awards. Also in 1993, he received Lifetime Achievement awards from the **R & B** Foundation Pioneer Awards and from Black Owned Broadcasters.

Now in his 70s, James continues to perform. He performs nearly 150 days a year, and he always draws a good audience. He uses many of his shows to raise money for good causes. He also tries to give a performance every year on his birthday.

James represented soul music at the June 29, 2001 celebration honoring black music. He is shown here with President George W. Bush.

He also continues to mix his music and his beliefs. In the 1990s, he spoke out against the school shootings in the United States. He wrote the song "Killing Is Out. School Is In." He still believes that education and business ownership are the keys to a better life. He encourages young people to use their talents and work to their full potential. He overcame difficulties in life, and he sees himself as an example for all people.

James's hits have set records. He has had the most **R & B** hits of all time. There have been more than 116 hits in the course of his career. He also charted 96 pop hits on the Top 100 charts. Numbers cannot say enough about James Brown, though. His genius and his heart are preserved through his music. The legend of James's music and his social causes lives on.

In his own words

"I worked on a job with my feet and my hands
But all the work I did
was for the other man
Now we demand a chance
to do things for ourselves
we're tired of beatin' our head against the wall
And workin' for someone else."
(From the song, "I'm Black and I'm Proud," 1969.)

Glossary

agent   person who takes care of a performer's business, such as getting record deals, so that the artist can concentrate on music and performances

amateur   person, usually a performer, who is not professional, or making much money, at what he or she is doing

booking company   agency that sets dates and places for performances

civil rights   rights of all U.S. citizens to fair and equal treatment under the law

Civil Rights Movement   name given to the long fight to gain civil rights for African Americans

funk form of African-American music focused on rhythm and improvisation. Each instrument plays different rhythms, instead of having some instruments play melody and harmony while only the drum and bass play rhythm. The music is very danceable.

gospel form of religious music started by African Americans in the rural South. Gospel combines traditional church music with African-American musical styles.

improvise   to invent at the moment

integrate   to include all people, regardless of color. The act of integrating is integration.

jazz   form of music developed by African Americans, based on improvisation, solos, and changing rhythms

juvenile detention center   place where teenagers, and sometimes children, who get in trouble with the law are sent. Similar to a prison.

protest   when a group of people gathers to voice their dislike for something or someone

record charts   system to keep track of the popularity of songs
rhythm   steady beat in a piece of music

rhythm and blues (R & B)   form of fast dance music developed by African Americans in the cities. Rhythm and blues music uses a full band, including drum, piano, bass, and electric guitar.

riot   when a large group of people gets out of control and becomes violent, usually because they are upset with something

segregate   to keep separate. Laws of **segregation** in the South unfairly kept black people away from white people.

soul music   music combining elements of jazz, gospel, and rhythm and blues. For many African Americans, soul music showed pride in black roots and culture.

sponsor   to support someone, often with food, shelter, or money

supervisors   people in charge of other people

Timeline

1933:	James Joe Brown Jr. is born.
1944:	James wins his first amateur talent contest.
1946:	James starts his own band called the Cremona Trio.
1949:	James gets arrested for stealing. He is placed in a juvenile detention center.
1952:	James is released. He begins to sing and perform gospel music.
1953:	James marries his first wife, Velma Warren.
1956:	James's first song, "Please Please Please," is released.
1957:	James takes over the performances scheduled for Little Richard.
1958:	"Try Me," his first number one hit on the R & B charts, is released.
1959:	James makes his first appearance at the Apollo Theater.
1963:	The tremendously popular album *Live at the Apollo* is released.
1965:	"Papa's Got a Brand New Bag" is released. It spends eight weeks at number one on the R & B charts. The song makes it to the top ten on the pop music charts.
1966:	James starts his Don't Be a Dropout campaign.
1968:	Martin Luther King Jr. is killed on April 4. Riots break out across the country.
1968:	James buys his first radio station in Knoxville, Tennessee.
1968:	James releases "I'm Black and I'm Proud" and "America Is My Home." These songs create problems between James and his audience.
1968:	Ben Bart, James's manager, dies. Syd Nathan of King Records also dies.
1970:	James marries his second wife, Deirdre. They have two daughters.
1973:	James's oldest son, Teddy, dies in a car accident.
1973:	Bobby Byrd, James's old friend and band mate, leaves the band.
1970s:	James ties with Elvis for the most charted pop hits. They both have 38.
1980:	James appears in *The Blues Brothers*.
1986:	James records the Grammy award-winning song "Living in America" for the movie *Rocky IV*. A new generation of music listeners is introduced to James.
1986:	James is among the first ten musicians in the Rock and Roll Hall of Fame.
1992:	James receives a Lifetime Achievement Award at the 34th Annual Grammy Awards.
2003:	James turns 70 years old.

Further Information

Further reading

Flanders, Julian, Ed. *The Story of Music: Gospel, Blues, and Jazz. Volume 5.* Danbury, Conn: Grolier Educational, 2001.

Grimbly, Shona, Ed. *The Story of Music: From Rock and Pop to Hip-Hop. Volume 6.* Danbury, Conn.: Grolier Educational, 2001.

Vernell, Marjorie. *Leaders of Black Civil Rights.* Farmington, Mich.:Gale Group, 2000.

Addresses

Rock and Roll Hall of Fame Foundation
1290 Avenue of the Americas
New York, New York 10104
Write here to find out who else is in the Rock and Roll Hall of Fame and how the artists are chosen.

The Children's Music Network
P.O. Box 1341
Evanston, IL 60204-1341
This organization works to make creative, diverse music for children. Write here for more information about what it is doing.

Index